IMPOSSIBLE TESTS

PREQUEL TO THE SHORTEN CHRONICLES

ROSALIND TATE

IMPOSSIBLE TESTS

Monday, 7ᵗʰ September 2015. England.
Hadley School.

'It's huge.' Isha scanned the airy circular room that took up the entire top floor of the stone turret.

'I wonder why it's called the Lair?' Sophie tilted her head back to see the vaulted ceiling, criss-crossed with curved, exposed beams. 'It's not a supervillain's HQ.'

'Much more exciting.' Isha grinned. 'Common room for year twelve and thirteen. Hormone central … with fit boys!'

'I wish,' said Sophie, stepping aside to

avoid a gangly, pug-faced youth pushing past her.

Golden autumnal light spilling through arched, leaded windows on three sides of the tower, softened the mismatched dog-eared armchairs, the angular lines of a snooker table and an ancient granite fireplace. On the wall was a three-foot long Tudor tapestry, depicting boys in doublet and hose lounging in idyllic countryside. Encased in a battered frame, faded and obscured by thick Perspex, it contrasted oddly with a shiny health and safety notice next to it: red letters stark on a white background.

Sophie sat on an oversized brown sofa and breathed in a musty smell of old stone and a richer scent from the seasoned oak planks on the floor.

'So glad you got the grades.' Isha flopped down beside her as more students came in.

Sophie nodded. To hide her discomfort, she bent forward to take off one of her navy pumps to remove an imaginary fragment of grit. She hadn't got the required GCSE grades to study for A levels but no other student knew that, not even Isha.

Five years ago, Sophie had won Hadley's prestigious George Eliot prize, a scholarship that paid all her school fees. For a scholar not to stay on for A levels was unheard of, so the headmistress, Miss Parncutt, had convened a confidential governors' meeting to justify Sophie's place, explaining that her exam results stemmed from the trauma in 2011 of losing her parents, not a lack of ability. And the governors had reluctantly agreed — just this once — to make an exception.

'Comfy as our favourite sofa in Ada.' Isha plumped up a tartan cushion.

Ada House with its cosy sitting room and shared dorms had been a much-loved sanctuary. But it felt good to be joining Lefroy, the senior house, along with students from another girls' house *and* the boys' houses.

Sophie leaned back against a softer, velvet cushion. 'Furniture … is up to expectations.' Banter was a good cover for nerves.

'Watch out, Lefroy,' said Isha, her voice melodramatic. 'I'm prepared.'

Be Prepared, or *Semper Paratus*, had been

the school motto for centuries, way before it was adopted by the Boy Scouts.

'I'm prepared too.' Ignoring a fresh flutter of anxiety, Sophie copied Isha's confident slouch.

They were both wearing navy pencil skirts, matching jackets, pale blue shirts and red ties. Boys wore the same except for navy trousers. The suits distinguished them from younger pupils who wore grey trousers or skirts and red blazers.

The room was filling up, the level of excited chatter rising.

'Incoming,' whispered Isha.

Sophie didn't look round. She didn't need to. She could hear Madison the Bitch Queen chatting animatedly with posh boy Hugo. Alex the Joker would be with them. The annoying trio were inseparable.

'Hugo made prefect,' whispered Isha.

Sophie rolled her eyes.

'I think he's fit.' Isha shot her a wicked grin. 'In a conventional, Robert Pattinson, sort of way.'

Sophie snorted. 'In the dark, maybe.' Despite the buzz of so much chatter, she could easily distinguish Hugo's clipped, English vowels jarring with Madison's Californian drawl... Sophie shut out his voice. She'd had years of practice.

Lily walked briskly towards them, her black, frizzy hair bouncing with each stride. A year older, Sophie's kickboxing partner was breezy, self-assured and popular.

Isha and Sophie stood and hugged her before sitting down again.

'Welcome to the Lair.' Lily sat on the arm of the sofa.

'Congrats on making head girl,' said Isha.

Lily self-consciously touched the badge on her lapel. 'I'm not used to it yet.'

'So much power...' said Sophie. 'I'll never win a bout again.'

'That would be good.' Lily smiled.

Isha lowered her voice. 'How does it work, with *everyone* hanging out here?'

'Works fine,' said Lily. 'There's plenty of space.'

The Lair and attached residential halls were much larger than the other houses.

And the tower was centuries older, with thicker walls and heavy oak doors, gridded with iron studs. Founded in 1545, Hadley was part castle, part stately home, except for a modern sports complex which was all glass and sharp angles.

Sophie tapped on her phone and showed Lily a photo that her Aunt Wendy had sent. Isha had already seen it.

'She's adorable,' said Lily, peering at the photo of Charlotte, Sophie's labradoodle puppy. 'And big. How old is she?'

'Five months. She's had a mega growing spurt.' And Sophie missed her like crazy.

'Hi, mind if I join you?' Peter Watson sat down languidly on a red sofa opposite.

The three girls focused *all* their attention. Peter was ridiculously good-looking: auburn wavy hair, chiselled cheekbones, rich brown eyes and thick black eyelashes any girl would have died for.

'This is good, isn't it?' he said.

'Yes,' simpered Isha.

Sophie ransacked her brain for something to say and came up empty.

'There's a new café opened in the village.' Pete smiled at Sophie, showing off his film-star teeth. 'Would you like to join me for lunch there on Saturday?'

'Love to,' Sophie managed to say.

'I'll meet you at the gates at noon.'

Sophie just nodded, not keen to push her luck with any more talking. She was in shock.

He unhurriedly stood up, gave the girls another breathtaking smile and sauntered off.

'No way,' said Lily.

Despite his ultra-fit status, Pete hadn't dated anyone at school. Well, until now.

'Go, girl,' mouthed Isha.

Sophie shook her head, shock giving way to excitement.

The week passed in a blur of new classes. Sophie had chosen straightforward subjects she enjoyed — Film Studies, Physical Education and English Literature — so she coped and began to relax.

But then it was Saturday.

Sophie walked down the drive, her heart

hammering. It had only taken three hours to decide what to wear: jeans, a pink cotton shirt and a classy faux leather jacket borrowed from Isha.

Pete was leaning against a tall pillar by the entrance studying his phone. He was also wearing jeans, paired with a black and white check shirt.

Act cool. 'Hi.'

'Hi.' He pocketed his phone. 'You look nice.'

She'd applied a hint of lip plumper. 'Thanks.'

They walked in companionable silence along the lane. This was fortunate, as Sophie's capacity for conversation seemed to have taken a permanent hike.

The café was small and clean and smelled of coffee and freshly baked bread. Sophie ordered tea and an egg sandwich. Good. Nerves were jangling but she could still speak. As she paid for her lunch, Pete ordered a coffee and a BLT and the girl behind the counter blushed, her colour rising as she scribbled on her pad.

'I'll bring your sandwiches over,' smiled

the girl, watching Pete under her lashes. He smiled back.

They sat by the window and while Sophie sipped tea, Pete showed her a video on his phone: a car driving along a racetrack. 'The latest Formula One Ferrari. The new short nose design helps with airflow underneath. They've kept last year's front wing, as well the blown front axle. The shape of the chassis is now higher and straighter, with a vanity panel intended for a future S-duct solution...'

Why the hell was he talking about this?

When the waitress put their sandwiches on the Formica table, Sophie said, 'I'm into slow knitting.'

He stared.

'Kidding.'

He hesitated. 'Sorry, got carried away. This is my passion.' He met her eyes.

Her insides melted, but in a good way. She forced herself not to simper. 'Watching, not driving?'

He shot her a sheepish smile. 'Not passed my test yet.' He told her about his Italian roots on his mother's side and then his gym routine — in mind-numbing detail.

Sophie said, 'Uh-huh' a lot, interspersed with 'Wow.'

'We could do this again next week,' said Pete, as they walked back to school.

'I'd like that,' said Sophie. They might kiss … she'd kissed other boys, but with Pete, it would be amazing.

~

Two Days Later. Monday, 14th September 2015.

'Pete and Sophie Arundel are an item,' said Madison, in her usual, library undertone.

'Mmm?' said Hugo, glancing up from a quadratic equation. He'd been staring at it for the last five minutes … still made no sense.

They were sitting in their usual alcove, in the oldest part of the library. Once a monastery, the secluded niches were big enough for two. Perfect for study — and gossip.

The comforting scent of old paper and ink usually helped Hugo work, but he struggled with maths—

'He is gorgeous.'

'Who is?'

'Pete Whatsisface,' said Madison.

'What about him?'

'You're not listening. He and Arundel are together.' Madison closed her exercise book. 'It sucks we have to do this.' Like Hugo, she'd scraped a C grade at GCSE, so Maths Club was compulsory.

Hugo closed his book too and sighed. He couldn't compete with Pete. Actually, nobody could.

'It makes no sense,' said Madison. 'I mean, she's okay looking, but such a loser.'

'Sorry?'

'Scholars are supposed to be seriously clever but her grades in the Club test were embarrassing. I don't get it.'

'That maths paper was brutal.'

'What does he see in her?'

'Um...'

'All she does is javelin and kickboxing. How boring is that?'

Hugo shrugged. His obsession with Sophie Arundel was a very private problem. And Madison wouldn't understand. Why would she? He didn't understand it himself.

When he'd seen Sophie on that first day at Hadley, recognition had swept over him so intensely he'd caught his breath. Within seconds the sensation had faded, but its essence had remained with him ever since, always there, humming in the back of his brain. The way she smiled, wistfully or ruefully, or with such joy her whole face lit up. Her spiky forthrightness, the way she rocked back on her heels when she was thinking… Back in year seven, she'd been chatting with Isha in the breakfast queue, and he'd known before she made a face that the smell of bacon made her nauseous. *How* he'd known that, he had no idea.

But he liked bacon, and they were in different academic sets, and their friends didn't mix and that was that.

Except it wasn't.

He dreamed about her. And occasionally when he was happily focused on history prep or playing cricket, something would tug at the edge of his mind. Just a murmur. More like a nudge than a memory.

He opened his exercise book and reread the first line of the equation.

'She always wears that lame witch outfit for Halloween.' Madison giggled. 'Maybe she's put a spell on Pete—'

Hugo sensed someone in front of the alcove and glanced up. Isha was standing with her arms folded, giving them a stare that would have curdled a latte. She'd overheard.

'What?' Madison didn't do conciliatory.

Protecting his secret, Hugo stayed quiet, and Isha stalked off, her shoes snicking fainter and fainter on the flagstone floor until the sound died away.

No doubt heading straight to her BFF... Hugo rubbed his temple. He should have apologised — now any chance to change their opinion of him, how he regarded Sophie, was gone.

Irretrievably, like a memory just beyond reach.

~

Three Months later. Friday, 11th December 2015.

'*So* cool you're going to his parents' house.' Isha clapped her hands together and grinned.

They were in the driveway on the last day of term, waiting for the minibus that took students to the station.

'His parents don't come back from Estonia until tomorrow.' Sophie pushed down the handle on her tatty, wheeled suitcase. 'So, it's likely we'll … you know.' The rain was turning into sleet and Sophie fastened her coat over her long white shirt and black jeans.

'A big deal.' Isha looked serious.

Pete was coming towards them, past an admiring gaggle of girls. He strolled like Prince Harry on a walkabout. Regal but sincere.

'I'm excited,' whispered Sophie, 'but ... to be honest, he's a bit boring.'

Isha made a face. '*No* sympathy.'

On the train, Pete was mostly fixated with his phone, so Sophie scrolled through pictures of Charlotte and watched cute animal videos.

Pete's home was a modest two-storey house on a leafy street in Wiltshire. His parents were in the military, so the government paid most of his school fees. Not rich, not snobby. A regular guy.

But as Pete opened his front door, Sophie's heart started thumping. She made herself take deep breaths. She was doing the right thing. They were both seventeen, mature... And she'd been on the pill for over a month.

They walked in, Pete closed the front door and parked his case neatly to the side in the small hall. 'Anyone here?' After a moment, he took off his coat and started up the stairs. When she hesitated, he turned and smiled. 'Come on.'

She left her case and coat and followed him.

Predictably, Pete's bedroom walls were covered in posters of cars. Identical except different colours: red, white and black. And the duvet on his single bed carried on the theme. The room was tidy and smelled faintly of lemon polish, the way spaces do when they get cleaned but aren't lived in for a while.

Pete closed the door and they kissed. In a self-conscious hurry, they undressed and cuddled under the duvet. Urged on by the unforgiving dimensions of the narrow bed, Pete lay on top of her.

Sophie felt a sharp pain and grimaced. Was it supposed to hurt? *Fifty Shades* and all that—

'Are you okay?' Pete looked concerned. He never looked concerned.

'Fine.' It had to get better … or why would anyone do this?

He was moving inside her, and that didn't hurt, just felt weird.

'Nice,' he was murmuring. 'Really nice.' He gave a low grunt and lay still. Too still.

A scene from *Downton* played in Sophie's head. That foreign guy died having sex...

Pete gave a satisfied sigh and rolled away from her.

Good. Not dead.

He reached for his phone on a bedside table. 'Selfie?'

Creepy or what? She grabbed his phone and shoved it under a pillow. 'No.'

'Oh.' He seemed disappointed.

She smiled at him. 'Let's have a shower.'

'Together?'

'Shower separately. Dress. Then, *tasteful* selfie.' Sophie put on her best doe eyes. 'Could you make a cup of tea?'

He blinked, surprised. 'Of course.' He got out of bed, took a dressing gown that was hanging on the door and took his time slipping into it, entirely unembarrassed.

Sophie averted her eyes, awareness of her inadequacy jostling with bemusement and disappointment.

When he disappeared downstairs, she jumped off the bed, threw on her shirt, picked up her other clothes and hurried into the corridor to find a bathroom.

A locked door and fierce hot water from a shower restored her equilibrium. Somehow, she needed to keep her distance without hurting his feelings.

A migraine ... perfect. It could last the whole weekend.

~

Seven Months Later. Tuesday, 28th June 2016.

Hugo's phone pinged.

He was sitting on a bench with Alex by the main running track, watching keen students getting ready for Athletics Day.

Hugo looked at his phone. '*Landscape gardener, teacher, lecturer* … I've no interest in gardening or teaching. Maybe I filled the career form out wrong?'

Alex's phone had also pinged. 'No, I've got *teacher* and *lecturer* too … and *politician*. Let's think. Do I want to be economical with the truth all day and get trolled to death on twitter all night? I don't think so.' He gave Hugo an apologetic grimace. 'Sorry, that wasn't meant as a cheap shot at your father.'

'I know.' Hugo's father *was* a politician; he'd been a member of parliament for years. 'I've seen Dad's workload first-hand. Politics holds zero appeal.'

Alex pocketed his phone. 'So, what did you want to tell me?'

Hugo took a deep breath and tried to explain his fixation with Sophie. But ten seconds in, Alex interrupted.

'You feel you're mysteriously *connected* to her? I don't get it.'

'I've felt like this for years. Everything about her — how she moves, how she talks, the way her hair shines in the sunshine — I get this tingle of recognition.'

'The tingle's likely something else.' Alex opened a lemonade can.

'I'm serious,' said Hugo, already wishing he hadn't shared his inexplicable obsession. He sighed. 'The sensation's always there, whether I'm near her or not. Sometimes, it's a despairing feeling, like a bereavement, but the upshot is ... I *know* her because somewhere, somehow, we've been together.'

Alex frowned. 'In a previous life?'

'Okay, that's mental.'

'Have you ever actually spoken to her?'

'Yes,' said Hugo, 'in the dinner queue last year.'

'Okay ... how many words?'

'You're being picky. Six, no seven. I said

the mashed potato looked grey and yucky and she agreed.'

Alex frowned again. 'More talking might be a good first step.'

'You think I'm imagining it.'

'No. You're not an "imagining it" kind of guy. Perhaps she reminds you of someone, from a movie or a TV series?'

Hugo shook his head. 'Been through all that. Came up empty.'

'Talk of the devil.'

Sophie was running down the track in athletics kit: navy trainers and shorts and a white, aertex shirt. Hugo smiled at her as she passed but she didn't notice.

'Do you think she's got problems with her eyes? Chucking Pete after one weekend … it's possible.' Alex sipped his lemonade.

'Or I'm invisible.' Hugo pushed his dark fringe off his forehead and adjusted his sun-glasses. 'On the upside, I don't need a cloak.'

Alex prodded him in the arm.

'Ow.'

'You're one hundred per cent solid *and* visible.'

'You say anything to Madison and you're toast.'

Alex put up his hands in mock surrender, waving his can. 'Your secret's safe with me.' He took another swig of lemonade. 'Anyway, Mads wouldn't believe me. You know how she feels about our Soph.'

'I never got that. Maybe it's a girl thing?'

'Or a Mads thing.' Alex carefully placed the can on the ground and put on his shades. 'She can be a bit ... direct.'

'That's an American thing.' Madison had lived in the States until she was ten. 'How are you getting on with Phoebe?'

'So so. I might change tack, move on to boys.' Alex's eyes gleamed.

Even after six years, Hugo couldn't tell when his friend was joking. 'No harm in experimenting.'

On the far side of the track, Sophie had stopped running and was stretching — her wind down routine.

Alex took off his shades. 'Just talk to her. I don't understand why you haven't.'

'I've tried to, but I freeze.' Hugo sighed.

'It's as if it would break the spell — or whatever it is.'

'Okay, despair ... like someone's died. You'll be telling me next you *like* feeling like crap.'

Hugo hesitated. 'I do, sort of. It's hard to explain.' The sadness was part of the awareness, the need, the longing.

'You should try everything once,' said Alex, 'except incest and Morris Dancing.'

'Oscar Wilde?'

'Not sure, but whoever it was should have added masochism to the exceptions.'

Alex tapped on his phone and showed it to Hugo. 'For you my friend, there are plenty of fish in the sea.'

On the screen was a gorgeous brunette, in jeans and a black, designer shirt, with стиль signed on a turtleneck collar. Her eyes were an unusually deep blue.

'Who's that?'

'Ekaterina Antonova.' Alex announced the name like a stage show host. 'She's coming over from Saint Petersburg in September and she'll be here *all* next year.'

Hugo peered at the photo again. 'I'm

glad the exchanges are back on.' They'd stopped in 2014 after Russia had annexed Crimea. 'I wonder what the word on the collar means?'

Alex tapped on his phone. 'Style.' He grinned. 'Best you brush up your Russian.'

~

Two Months Later. Monday, 5th September 2016.

'Koldovstoretz.' A tall, thick-set boy gestured at the Lair.

Hugo googled on his phone. 'Russian Hogwarts ... this may look like Khogvarts — Hogwarts — but there's no magic.'

'But hotter girlz?' smiled the boy, his eyes on Madison.

'Much hotter.' Hugo apologetically acknowledged Madison who'd raised an eyebrow, irritated that they were talking *about* her, not to her.

Behind the boy was the girl from Alex's photo. Tall and leggy, in person she was even more striking. Hugo smiled at her and she returned the smile, revealing even, white teeth.

She stepped forward and peered at Hugo's badge. 'Meanz?'

'Head boy.'

'Top boy,' she said.

Her husky voice gave him goose bumps. 'Would you mind if I practised my Russian on you?'

Ekaterina smiled again. 'If I can practize English. Pact, yes?'

'Pact.' Hugo hesitated. *'Kakiye u tebya khobbi?'*

'Hobbies … I love chez.'

'Chess… I love acting and fencing.'

'Fenc…,' said Ekaterina. 'I don't know this word.'

Hugo pretended to fence with an imaginary rapier.

'I think we get on famously.'

Madison exchanged a glance with Alex that meant, 'Interesting.'

In the following weeks, even when he was supposed to be doing history or economics prep, Hugo worked on his conversational Russian with Ekaterina, closeted in the alcove in the library. But conversation in any language was minimal. Incompatible with kissing.

Madison and Alex — and the rest of the school — were impressed, but at the beginning of October, after breakfast, Alex drew Hugo aside.

'You're meeting Ekaterina?'

Hugo put on his smug face. 'My Russian's getting better every day.'

'Before you get in too deep...' Alex showed him a news article on his phone. *Daniil Antonov expands his business empire...*

'So?'

'Her father's one of Putin's inner circle. That's how he's kept his money. Putin's the richest man in the world but Antonov's not far behind.'

'How rich is rich?'

'Enough to buy a multi-national bank and another one,' said Alex. 'Many, many billions.'

A happy vision of making out with Ekaterina on an exclusive Caribbean island played in Hugo's mind.

'Obviously, you're a catch. Handsome,

impressive intellect...' Alex's sarcasm was legendary.

'But?'

'You need to be careful. With your father's day job, things could get complicated.'

Hugo's father had been promoted back in June, was now Foreign Secretary. 'Ekaterina … it's early days.' Hugo put his hand through his hair. 'Not serious.'

~

Two Months Later. Friday, 25th November 2016.

'Staying in one of her father's five-star hotels.' Alex flopped into a desk chair in Hugo's dorm. 'How is that, "Not serious?"' He gestured the quotation marks. 'When did she ask you?'

'After breakfast.' Hugo was sitting on his bed, reading a pocket version of *Conversational Russian, Quick and Easy*. 'My dad's okay with it.' He'd initially messaged his mother, but it was his father, recently returned from a climate change conference in

Morocco, who'd called him back. And given him his second warning to be careful. Hugo closed the book. 'It'll be fine.'

'Supplies?' Alex twirled a pencil in his fingers.

'Plenty.' 'Supplies' was their slang for condoms. Yes, he'd be careful. Hugo stood up and stretched. Not going home over an exeat weekend, the three-day break during term, would be a first, but in his last year at Hadley this was the right call—

'How are you getting there?'

'One of her family's chauffeurs is picking us up.' Even as Hugo said this, it felt unreal, like a movie. He checked his watch. 'Catch you later.' He grabbed his case and made his way to the school driveway.

Ekaterina was already there. 'That iz our vehicle.'

The Range Rover coming towards them was no different from other cars that dropped off and collected high profile foreign students. Black. Tinted windows. Armoured.

They got in the back and Hugo took a calming breath. The prospect of spending whole days — and two nights — with Eka-terina was deliciously exciting. Intoxicating. Her slim curves were barely concealed under an open, long cardigan, an expensive-looking thin top and a short skirt. He swallowed. He'd worn the wrong clothes. Navy chinos and a cream shirt were too casual…

They were wafted *very* safely into London and were greeted like royalty in the palatial reception of the hotel. Without waiting for them to sign a form or bother with anything as mundane as handing over a credit card, a uniformed flunkey carried their bags and escorted them into a lift.

Never a fan of enclosed spaces, even luxurious ones with beech-veneered walls, Hugo held his breath until the lift doors opened.

The top floor was hushed and the carpet along the corridor was so deep his heels sank into it.

Up ahead, two chambermaids were standing by a wagon filled with bath lotions and towels.

Ekaterina made imperial, shooing gestures with her hands and the girls jumped back against a wall as she passed, with Hugo and the flunkey in her wake.

Hugo stopped walking, turned around and mouthed, 'Sorry,' before catching up with Ekaterina.

The flunkey opened a door with a key-card, placed their small, wheeled cases carefully on a marble floor in an entrance hall and put two key-cards on a side table. 'Shall I unpack, madam?'

'No,' said Ekaterina. 'That iz all.'

The flunky left, and after the door shut behind him with a heavy clunk, Hugo said, 'You were out of order back there.'

She frowned, puzzled.

'Those girls. How do you think they felt when you shooed them like that?'

'Shoooed?'

Hugo copied her dismissing gesture.

'Oh.' She shrugged. 'Russian way.'

Leaving the cases, Hugo followed her through an internal door, unconvinced. More likely, the oligarch way.

He paused, realised his mouth was open, and shut it hastily. This wasn't like any hotel he'd ever stayed in.

Two enormous chandeliers, shaped like upside-down umbrellas, harshly illuminated a shiny, mahogany dining table laid for eight. Hugo walked past a large box-shaped metallic divider to a sitting room; a TV, fully six feet across, was set into the other side of the ugly box. He took in low-backed grey sofas and to his left, paperback spines in primary colours on plain, wooden bookshelves. Reminiscent of 1960s modernism, the bookcases contrasted oddly with the fancy chandeliers. And why were the lights even on, given that the windows overlooking Knightsbridge were floor-to-ceiling and all the cream blinds were up?

'Explore.' Ekaterina shot him a grin and disappeared through a door on the far side of the sitting room.

He went after her into a black granite bathroom, so vast it dwarfed a jacuzzi, a state-of-the-art shower and a roll-top bath with gold taps — built for two. A scent of jasmine and rose, and a deeper, musky aroma was swirling from three, recently lit candles, arranged in a candelabra on a shelf by the bath. Surreal.

Through another door was a spacious bedroom, also with faux 1960s furniture, except the bed was big enough for a football team. He lingered on the threshold, nerves swirling.

Ekaterina pouted. 'You don't like?'

So over the top, it was creepy. But he said, 'Amazing.'

Ekaterina lifted a bottle of champagne from an ice bucket on a table by a window, opened it with practised aplomb and carefully poured bubbly into two flutes.

Hugo accepted a glass. 'To you.' He clinked her glass and sipped. The champagne was richer, deeper than any he'd tasted. Not that he'd tasted much. Not the real stuff.

Ekaterina finished her drink in two gulps. 'We make out?'

'Er, yes. Where?' They were spoiled for choice.

'Start … conventional.' She pointed at the bed.

'Good idea.' He'd be okay, once he'd kissed her.

And he was.

She seemed happy, making kitten noises and afterwards they lay entangled, co-cooned in an endless cotton sea. Her skin, *so* soft, and the way she moved … pleasure after pleasure. Forget Sophie Arundel. Ekaterina was a revelation. Sensual, mysterious, addictive. He kissed her temple. In the coming months, he'd really get to know her, mind and soul. Take a lifetime––

'We could have buddle bath?'

Her accented voice still gave him goose bumps. 'I'm cosy right here.' He cast around on the side table for more supplies. She'd told him she was on the pill but he was being careful.

Supplies sorted, he kissed her again, heat pooled in his stomach and he surrendered to delicious sensation.

A while later he fell asleep, only waking as Ekaterina talked on the phone in low, fast Russian. Her voice carried softly through the bathroom door, pleasantly soporific, and he let the sound run over him, not trying to translate it, drifting in and out. '... *konferentsiya v Marrakesh … khorosho, ya sprashu ob otsye...*'

Ekaterina ended the call, padded into the room and Hugo felt her stretch out against him. His body reacted, completely waking him. 'Who was on the phone?'

'Dad. Checking I'm okay.'

Hugo smiled. His parents still worried about his older sisters, though they'd long ago left home.

Ekaterina ran a long, scarlet fingernail down his chest. 'He was checking you come from good family.'

That didn't add up. Her father would have checked on him — *and* his family — long before now. By all accounts, he was a thorough guy.

Ekaterina's lips were on his, her kiss sweet and inviting, and Hugo should have been lost in the moment, but her words on the phone were nagging at him. '...*konferentsiya v Marrakesh ... khorosho, ya sprashu ob otsye...*'

Something *Marrakesh*. A city in Morocco. *I'll ask about his father...* yes, that was what she'd said. Alex's warning repeated in his head. *With your father's day job, things could get complicated.*

No, this was paranoia. Just ask her. 'Was your father asking about *my* father?' His voice came out breathy.

She tensed so fleetingly, he almost missed it. 'No,' she whispered against his cheek.

And then he realised. *Konferentsiya* meant conference. Even as he trailed kisses on Ekaterina's neck, his brain was dredging up a Cabinet briefing note he'd glanced at in the summer holidays. His usually meticulous father, distracted by a phone call from the prime minister, had left it on the kitchen table.

Classification: Secret. United Nations Climate Change Conference. Marrakesh, Morocco, 7–18 November 2016 ... Putin is exploiting American indecision in the region, increasing Morocco's dependence on Russia, pushing for new arms deals...

His father had snatched the paper away, joking that the conference was 'less about climate change, more a gathering of spies manoeuvring for advantage.'

Was Ekaterina's father telling her to fish

for anything the British Foreign Secretary — his father — might have let slip?

She'd just lied to him. So, yes.

No point in asking the same question. Or different ones. Whatever reassurances or excuses she came up with, he wouldn't believe her.

He stopped kissing. Making out in a luxury hotel was one thing but compromising his father's career, reputation... He rolled away from her. 'I'm sorry, I need time to think. I know your father's put you in an awkward position.'

'Pozition?'

No point in sugar coating it. 'Asking you to spy for him.'

'*Shto?*'

He jumped out of bed and Ekaterina sat up, grabbing at the duvet to cover her chest. 'You talk *khuynya*. You don't know him.'

His clothes were in a jumble on the floor. He pulled on his underpants.

Ekaterina let the duvet drop. 'Come to bed.'

He focused on getting his socks on. 'Sorry,' he repeated, hauling up his chinos and fastening them.

'*Yoptel-mopsel.*' A stream of Russian expletives exploded from Ekaterina's mouth. '*Nu naher.*'

He stepped into his shoes and fumbled into his shirt. He managed to fasten one button and gave up. 'Got to go.'

Ekaterina leaped off the bed, pulled on her long cardigan, tied it closed and started shouting — Russian mixed in with English swearing.

He'd never seen anyone lose their temper so completely. All control gone. He rushed through the bathroom, sitting room, dining room and finally reached the hall, but Ekaterina was close behind him, her tirade getting louder.

His shirt was inside out. He gave up on fastening it, grabbed his suitcase, hauled open the door and scurried down the corridor, a diatribe of outraged Russian following him to the lift.

~

He turned his key in the lock and pushed open the front door.

His mother was in the hall. 'Are you all right?'

He stepped inside, saw his messy hair in the hall mirror and tried to flatten it. 'Fine. I just need to tell you something.' The fifteen-minute Uber ride to Wimbledon had given him time to calm down, decide what to do.

His mother reached up and hugged him and he hugged her back. At seventeen, he was a six foot three beanpole. Young enough *not* to want to confide in his parents, but old enough to know he had to.

In the kitchen, Edward Harrington was leaning against the Aga cooker, sipping tea and reading something on his phone. He looked up, surprised.

Hugo's mouth dried. 'Hello.' The greeting came out too quiet, sheepish. He reluctantly met his father's eyes.

'You're in a state.' Edward gestured at the table. 'Sit down.'

'There's fresh tea in the pot.' His mother took mugs from a cupboard.

His father sat opposite him and Hugo

drew a deep breath and told them about the phone call.

'Antonov's people will have compiled a brief about us from public sources.' His father narrowed his eyes. 'How would you describe your relationship with Ekaterina?'

'Serious,' said Hugo, flatly. He'd been fooling himself, pretending otherwise.

His mother put two steaming mugs of tea on the table and sat down. 'Does Ekaterina feel the same?'

'I think so,' said Hugo. 'Well, she did until I bailed.'

'Perhaps why Antonov went fishing early?' said Edward Harrington, half to himself.

'Actually, I think asking questions for her father might be … normal. She knew I'd caught her out but didn't understand why I had to leave.' Hugo looked at his father. 'Why didn't you warn me?'

'If you remember, I said Ekaterina didn't need to know every detail about our family.'

Hugo sighed. 'Too subtle, Dad.'

'What I hadn't anticipated,' added Edward, 'was that Antonov would push so soon, be so blatant.'

Hugo stared into his tea. 'I was surprised you agreed to me going.'

His parents exchanged a look that Hugo recognised. They were wondering how honest they should be.

'We were ... concerned.' His mother sipped her tea. 'But if we'd said no, how would you have reacted?'

'Asked again, after Christmas.'

Fiona Harrington smiled. 'Been even more determined, got in deeper.'

Hugo shot her a rueful smile. His mother should have studied psychology, not law.

~

Seven Months Later. Saturday, 24 June 2017.

Hadley's sports complex was crowded, hot and noisy.

Students from another school — Wycliffe College — had been bussed in to cheer for their girl in the Kickboxing County Final and were shouting themselves hoarse to be heard over the home contin-

gent, who were yelling. 'So-phie,' in a sing-
song chant.

'Come on, Sofia.' Ekaterina's yell was
lost in the general din. She turned and
smiled at Hugo who was seated three rows
behind her, and he smiled back. A week
after he'd left the hotel, they'd met by
chance on the way to the Lair and she'd
made the first move to make up. 'It iz diffi-
cult, with my father,' was all she'd said.

But it was a sort of apology, and Hugo
had pretended he'd over-reacted, feeling a
perverse mix of regret and relief. He was
fairly sure she'd always dutifully asked her
mates questions, so it had been natural to
do the same with him — her first proper
boyfriend. Yes, he was probably still on
Antonov's radar, but of less interest.

Hugo turned his attention to the kickboxing ring and the Wycliffe girl and Sophie warming up in their respective
corners. But as he watched them stretching
and throwing air punches, he swayed,
fighting off nausea, and gripped the sides of
his seat. The sports complex always
smelled of sweat, despite ferocious air-con-

ditioning, and today that was souring his throat. He'd been ill with glandular fever two months ago; he'd thought he was over it.

Madison touched his arm. 'You need to rest. We should go to the Lair.'

Not far away, someone propped open a door, letting in fresh air. Hugo breathed hard and closed his eyes. 'I'll be okay in a minute.'

'Sure?'

He nodded.

'Come on, Sophie,' hollered Alex.

'She can't win,' said Madison.

Alex snorted. 'I wouldn't bet on it.'

'What's happening?' Hugo opened his eyes.

'Nothing,' said Alex. 'Not started yet.'

'The semi-final this morning was disappointing.' Madison frowned. 'No slow-motion leaps and kicks.'

Alex grinned. 'You've watched too many superhero movies.' He gave a piercing wolf-whistle.

In the centre of the hall, still in her corner, Sophie was sweating, slowing her breathing, her instructor's mantra repeating in her head. *Assess, opportunity, pounce.*

Assess. Fran, her opponent, was sinewy, had a flat, taut stomach, muscular arms, and at five foot eleven, was six inches taller. Famous for her quick knock-outs, her punches had a notoriously long reach. So did her kicks. And she'd just made the national team.

Opportunity. Fran had never seen Sophie Arundel fight, might underestimate how quick she was.

Pounce. Use the Sophie killer feint. Had always worked before, but Fran was in a different league—

The bell rang for the first bout.

Five minutes seemed to pass in seconds, Sophie's heart beating loud in her ears, blocking, dodging, near hits, not quick enough, too fast, too hard.

In the short break, Sophie sat in her corner, panting but relieved. Still here. She'd already lasted longer than most people did against Fran.

The bell rang and Sophie jumped to her feet.

Up in the stand, surrounded by yelling and stamping, Hugo was silently willing Sophie to win but also didn't want the match to end. Being able to openly watch her like this, minute by minute, felt illogically illicit. A stupid, guilty pleasure.

Fran feinted and landed a clean kick on Sophie's thigh, dodging so Sophie couldn't do a counter-kick, let alone punch. Hugo groaned and shook his head.

Sophie got in a kick during the next bout, but so did Fran.

In the fourth round, a phone flashed in Fran's eyes, giving Sophie time to deliver a solid punch, but in the last bout, clinching set in. Hugo chewed his lip. The longer they grappled, the smaller the chance that Sophie could somehow win.

Sophie stepped back, out of Fran's reach, desperately trying to focus. She'd deliberately not used her best feinting move but time was running out. Come on, Fran, hesitate, just for an instant. *Any* opening, however slight...

Seconds raced by. Now or never. Sophie feinted to the right and kicked with her left leg, landing a blow on Fran's knee, followed by a punch that caught Fran on the arm.

Then the bell rang.

The girls left the ring and stood together while the three judges consulted.

In the stand, Hugo had lost count of rounds won or lost, but knew it was close. The spectators quietened but after five minutes grew restless, 'Go, Fran,' competing with, 'So-phie.'

Fran exhaled. 'The panel don't normally take this long.'

Sophie nodded, just wanted it over.

After more long minutes, the senior judge from the British Kickboxing Council stood up, his bald pate shiny in the arena's overhead lights, and the spectators went quiet. 'This was a high-quality contest and I congratulate you both. By a *very* slight margin, 49 to 48 points, the winner is ... Sophie Arundel.'

Hugo leapt to his feet, Alex and Madison started yelling, and the whole hall erupted with cheers and catcalls.

'I got lucky,' said Sophie to Fran, as they shook hands. She wasn't being modest. Fran was stronger as well as taller — and now knew all her moves.

Someone shouted, 'You were robbed,' as Fran hurried towards the Wycliffe students, and Sophie ran over to the Hadley cohort, who were still whooping and shouting.

'You've achieved the impossible.' Isha hugged her.

'It was hard.'

'I don't mean the match,' said Isha. 'Look.'

Alex was clapping, even Madison was smiling.

'*Every* clique was rooting for you. You've united the whole school.' Isha caught Sophie's disbelieving expression and laughed. 'It won't last. But good one.' They high-fived.

Hugo was giving her a thumbs-up sign and Sophie found herself grinning at him. Yes, even posh boy Hugo had been rooting for her. Their eyes locked and for a moment she felt giddy. Okay, too much adrenalin and now it was seeping away.

But inside Hugo, butterflies were performing a rap-dance. He was no longer invisible. Elation ran through him, so pure and fierce, it took him by surprise.

'There'll be a good party tonight. Mr J's even authorised a miniscule amount of beer.' Alex pretended to punch Hugo's arm. 'And you ... need to seize the moment.'

Outside, Ekaterina was waiting for him.

'I saw ... before the metch. You are still sick,' she said, as they walked to the Lair.

'I'll be okay,' said Hugo. 'It was just so crowded in there.'

She nodded.

He still liked Ekaterina. Actually, felt sorry for her. But the other feelings had dissolved when Sophie's eyes had met his. Like a magic spell.

An hour later, on the far side of the Lair common room, Sophie joined in self-consciously with a boisterous rendition of Queen's *We Are The Champions* but stayed close to Isha, as if connected by invisible string. And she was determinedly not looking in Hugo's direction.

His butterflies had been replaced by a familiar, hollow feeling and he stayed where he was, flanked by Alex and Madison. The moment had passed.

'She just needs a nudge,' whispered Alex, as they finished their beer. 'The Leaving Ball will be another chance.'

~

Two Weeks Later. Saturday, 8th July 2017.

'Thiz party is pretty,' Ekaterina gestured at the splendid Tudor hall, decked out with balloons and elegant, round tables laid for dinner. Angelic in a long white diamante dress, her hair was arranged in soft waves.

Hugo smiled. 'It is.' The Leaving Ball was a big deal. Most parents attended, some flying in from the other side of the planet.

When Ekaterina had confirmed her parents were coming to the Leaving Ball, Hugo had phoned home, worried his father might avoid Antonov by not coming too.

'I won't seek him out,' said Edward, 'but being in the same room isn't a problem.'

Hugo glanced towards the hall entrance.

Sophie was there with Isha, talking with Pete Whatsisface. Evidently still friends.

Sophie's floor-length slinky blue dress showed off her delicate figure and complemented her blonde hair. Isha was Bollywood colourful in an emerald sari and long, embroidered sash. But Pete in black tie looked surreal. Like a photoshopped model.

'Hey.' Alex was striding between the tables, smart not surreal.

'Penguin suit suits you,' said Hugo. 'You should wear black tie more often.'

'Hope to.' Alex crossed his fingers. 'Grades permitting, Oxford will be party central.'

Hugo's parents arrived and his mother kissed him on the cheek.

She smiled. 'You're properly better.'

'Yes.' He accepted a glass of Prosecco from a waitress and took a sip. He'd been signed off as fit in June to sit his A levels but still felt tired. He'd bail before midnight.

On the other side of the hall, Ekaterina had disappeared inside a huge, paternal bear hug.

Daniil Antonov's dark hair was cut close

to the scalp and his neat moustache and goatee framed a hard mouth. He was slightly overweight, but his smooth, calculated steps suggested a high level of fitness, maybe a background in the military.

Ekaterina was now talking excitedly, exuding an air of entitled innocence, while her father carefully scanned the hall.

Hugo had no wish to catch his eye. He smiled at his own father and pointed to a table. 'We're over there.'

They'd been seated with Madison, Alex and their parents, as far from the Antonovs as possible. This hadn't happened by chance. The headmistress not only knew every pupil by name, their backgrounds, their individual strengths and weaknesses. Miss Parncutt also had an impressive grasp of diplomacy and international relations.

After everyone finished a salmon starter, Madison held up her wine glass. 'To spreading our wings.'

They all clinked glasses.

'And this isn't the end,' said Alex. 'We'll meet up in September.'

'We'll get the grades.' But Madison's tone

was equivocal, and Hugo shot her a reassuring smile.

After the meal, Alex stood up, his eyes alight with mischief. 'Let's go outside, hit the dodgems. Be warned, I've passed my driving test.' The bravado in his voice was tinged with relief.

Hugo recognised the feeling. He'd somehow managed to pass, despite feeling under par.

'Be scared, boys. I'm licenced to drive on *two* continents.' Madison got to her feet, her chair scrapping on the floor.

'I'll catch you up,' said Hugo.

When they'd tired of dodgems, they'd move on to dancing, roulette with jelly babies for prizes, and finally — near midnight — enjoy a fireworks display. Their parents, though, were happily chatting and drinking coffee, making no move to leave the table.

As his friends reached the exit, Hugo stood and walked towards Sophie.

She was sitting at a table in the middle of the room with Isha, chatting to a middle-aged woman in a navy and gold sari and a grey-haired man in black tie: Isha's parents.

Also at the table was a tired-looking woman in a cream trouser suit, seated in a wheelchair.

'Hello, I'm Hugo.' He smiled at the lady in the wheelchair.

She brushed a strand of hair from her eyes and smiled back. Her bobbed hair was the exact same shade of blonde as Sophie's. 'I'm Wendy Higgins. Sophie's aunt. Very pleased to meet you.'

He shook her hand. Sophie's parents must be abroad, or just busy. He turned to Sophie. 'I've been meaning to say, the kick-boxing final was really cool.'

Something showed in her face. Puzzlement? 'Thanks.'

'Shall we hit the roulette?' Isha got to her feet.

Still looking puzzled, Sophie stood up too. 'See you later.'

As they scuttled away, Wendy frowned, embarrassed.

To cover the silence, Hugo said, 'Nice to meet you,' and turned on his heel. Alex had been right last year. This obsession was weird — and masochistic. Time to move on.

Outside, Alex and Madison were waiting in a queue by the dodgems. Taller than Alex in her high heels, Madison's close-fitting red dress complemented her shapely figure and shiny dark hair. And with her vibrant, scarlet lipstick, she was Hollywood gorgeous.

Hugo sensed she'd wanted more than friendship for a while, and with Sophie's snub fresh in his mind, when he reached Madison, he drew her close. She tilted her head, her lips near his, and he kissed her softly, then urgently, ignoring Alex's sarcastic whooping.

'I wish I wasn't flying to the States tomorrow,' she said, when he finally pulled away.

He could have offered to fly out to her mother's place, but he needed to do *nothing* in the holidays. Get completely better. 'We'll meet up in Oxford.'

Madison smiled. 'We could do the dodgems later.'

'His room's a tip,' said Alex, grinning from ear to ear.

'You could help me finish packing.' Hugo

managed to keep a straight face but only just.

Alex gave them a lazy salute before climbing into a dodgem car, and Madison and Hugo, trying to look casual, strolled towards the Lair's residential hall.

Still dressed up, Sophie sat on her bed in the dorm and smiled at Isha. 'Fab party.'

'The best.' Isha perched on a chair, shucked off her shoes and wiggled her toes.

'But Hugo introducing himself,' said Sophie, 'that was strange.'

Isha shot Sophie an impish grin. 'I know you felt uncomfortable when he just walked up, but perhaps he likes you?'

'Or had too much to drink.'

'Which reminds me...' Isha opened her evening bag and extracted a small Prosecco bottle.

'You stole that from our table,' said Sophie, in mock horror.

'Might have done.' Isha stood up in bare feet and put the bottle on Sophie's desk. 'It doesn't feel real, does it? Our last day at school. Ever.'

'I know.' Sophie yawned. 'But I can visit you in Oxford.'

'Definitely.' Isha pushed out her bottom lip. 'As long as I get the grades…'

'You will.' Isha's scores in the mocks had been near perfect. '*No* idea how I've done.'

'What's your fallback choice?'

'Somewhere in Derbyshire.' Sophie made a face. 'Miles away.'

Isha twisted off the bottle cap and poured Prosecco into two plastic tumblers.

Sophie accepted a cup and smiled. 'To new adventures.'

~

Five Weeks later. Thursday, 17 August 2017.

Hugo left a mug of coffee on the kitchen table and opened an email on his phone, worrying it was spam. But it wasn't. *Congratulations on choosing our prestigious social history course…*

His stomach dropped. He hadn't received notification of his grades but this automated email had been triggered from a university in Derbyshire because he *hadn't* got three A stars.

He'd lost his place at Oxford.

After a long moment, he sat at the table and forced himself to read the whole email. A year ago, he'd taken less than a minute to choose his fallback choice. Never imagined he'd go there.

A new email popped up. He clicked and gulped. *Economics: E, History: E, Russian: D.* He put his head in his hands.

Breathe.

He took a sip of now tepid coffee and Googled the provincial university: decent reputation for I.T. but ranked bottom for research and alumni salaries.

He stood up and walked to the French windows that overlooked the garden, not seeing the trees and flowers drenched in soft, summer rain, only picturing the snide glances and knowing nudges if he returned to Hadley. Repeated the whole year.

Why the hell hadn't he listened to Parncutt and deferred his exams? He'd known he wasn't better. Every single paper had been an impossible test.

Oxford might reconsider if he retook the exams … but he couldn't face it. Not now. Maybe not ever.

This other place might not be too bad. He'd know after a day, a week.

He sat at the table again, confirmed he'd take up the social history place, and messaged Alex and Madison his grades. He wiped his eyes and tapped out *bummer*, before pressing send. Banter helped with setbacks. He took another deep breath. Okay, not with this.

His phone pinged. Madison had texted, *Really sorry about your exams. What are you going to do? xxx*

It was three in the morning in LA. She must have stayed up for her results. He tapped rapidly. *I'll see how the other place pans out. You got the grades?*

Lucky.

I'll visit at weekends.

Can't wait. Miss you. xxx

His phone rang.

'Hello, mate,' said Alex.

Hugo swallowed. 'You got the grades?'

'Yeah. Are you okay?'

'I've been better.' He rubbed his forehead and repeated what he'd texted Madison.

As he ended the call, he heard the front door open in the hall. No need to act brave. He hadn't fooled his friends. Certainly wouldn't fool his mother.

The shock was wearing off and his brain was clearing. He smiled at his mother as she came into the kitchen. Yes, he'd be in Derbyshire during the week, but his weekends — and his future — still lay in Oxford.

With Madison.

AUTHOR'S NOTE

Just weeks after *Impossible Tests*, in *Stranded,* the first book of the *Shorten Chronicles*, Sophie falls with her dog though a door into the past, into a grand house a century ago. And Hugo falls through the door with her.

Join Sophie and Hugo's adventure (in large print, paperback, hardback, audiobook or ebook):

https://bookshop.rosalindtate.com

For news about current and future releases, go to:

www.rosalindtate.com

ABOUT THE READERS CLUB

The Readers Club exists so that you – my favourite person, the intelligent reader – can stay in touch with new *Shorten Chronicles* fantasy books, and any special promotions and discounts.

Just go to rosalindtate.com to join. You receive *Impossible Tests* (ebook and audiobook) for free. Those editions aren't available to anyone outside the Readers Club. It's for you in the Readers Club and no one else.

My way of saying thank you for reading my books.

Rosalind Tate lives in Gloucestershire, England. She served in the military, then worked as a journalist and a lawyer. She has three grown up children, a tolerant husband and two utterly gorgeous dogs.

Email Rosalind: rosalind@ rosalindtate.com

Let's chat about all things Shorten!

～

IMPOSSIBLE TESTS
Prequel to The Shorten Chronicles

First published in Great Britain in 2020
by TOB Publishing

Formatting by Vellum
Cover Design by 187Designz
Website by sprkdesign

TOB Publishing

Some kids ride
their bikes to school.
They are sure to
wear their helmets.

Kim lives far
from school.
She rides the bus
to school.

Tom lives far
from school.
He rides a bus
to school, too.

5

Some kids live
near school.
They <mark>could</mark> ride
their bikes to school.

Some kids ride the train to school. <mark>Maybe</mark> the train is late today.

Some kids walk
to school.
They get help
to cross the street.

Some kids go to
school by car.
They don't forget
about their seat belts.

Kids go to school
in many ways.
How do you
go to school?

Responding

Word Builder

What ways can you get to school?
Use the word "by" in your answer.

Write About It

Text to Self Draw a picture of
yourself going to school. Label
your picture: "by _____."

WORDS TO KNOW

about	don't
by	maybe
car	sure
could	there

TARGET STRATEGY **Visualize**

Picture what is happening as you read.